To Richard Thompson—
a big guy in my book

Printed in Singapore
Reinforced binding

First Edition
10 9 8 7 6 5 4 3
F850-6835-5-13243

Library of Congress Cataloging-in-Publication Data

Willems, Mo.
A big guy took my ball! / text and illustrations by Mo Willems.—1st ed.
p. cm.
Summary: Piggie is upset because a whale took the ball she found, but Gerald finds a solution that pleases all of them.
ISBN 978-1-4231-7491-2 (alk. paper)
[1. Elephants—Fiction. 2. Pigs—Fiction. 3. Whales—Fiction. 4. Animals—Fiction. 5. Friendship—Fiction. 6. Play—Fiction.] I. Title.
PZ7.W65535Big 2013
[E]—dc23 2012010899

Visit www.hyperionbooksforchildren.com
and www.pigeonpresents.com

Hyperion Books for Children
New York
AN IMPRINT OF DISNEY BOOK GROUP

A Big Guy Took My Ball!

Gerald!

I found a big ball,

and it was *so* fun!

And then a big guy came—

and—

and—

and—

HE
MY

TOOK BALL!

I am so upset.

That is not good.

That is not right!

Big guys have *all* the fun!

What about
the little guys!?

What makes those big guys think they are so big?!

Their size?

WELL, I AM
BIG TOO!

I will get your big ball from that big guy!

My
hero!

Here I go!

Let's see how big
this "big guy" is!

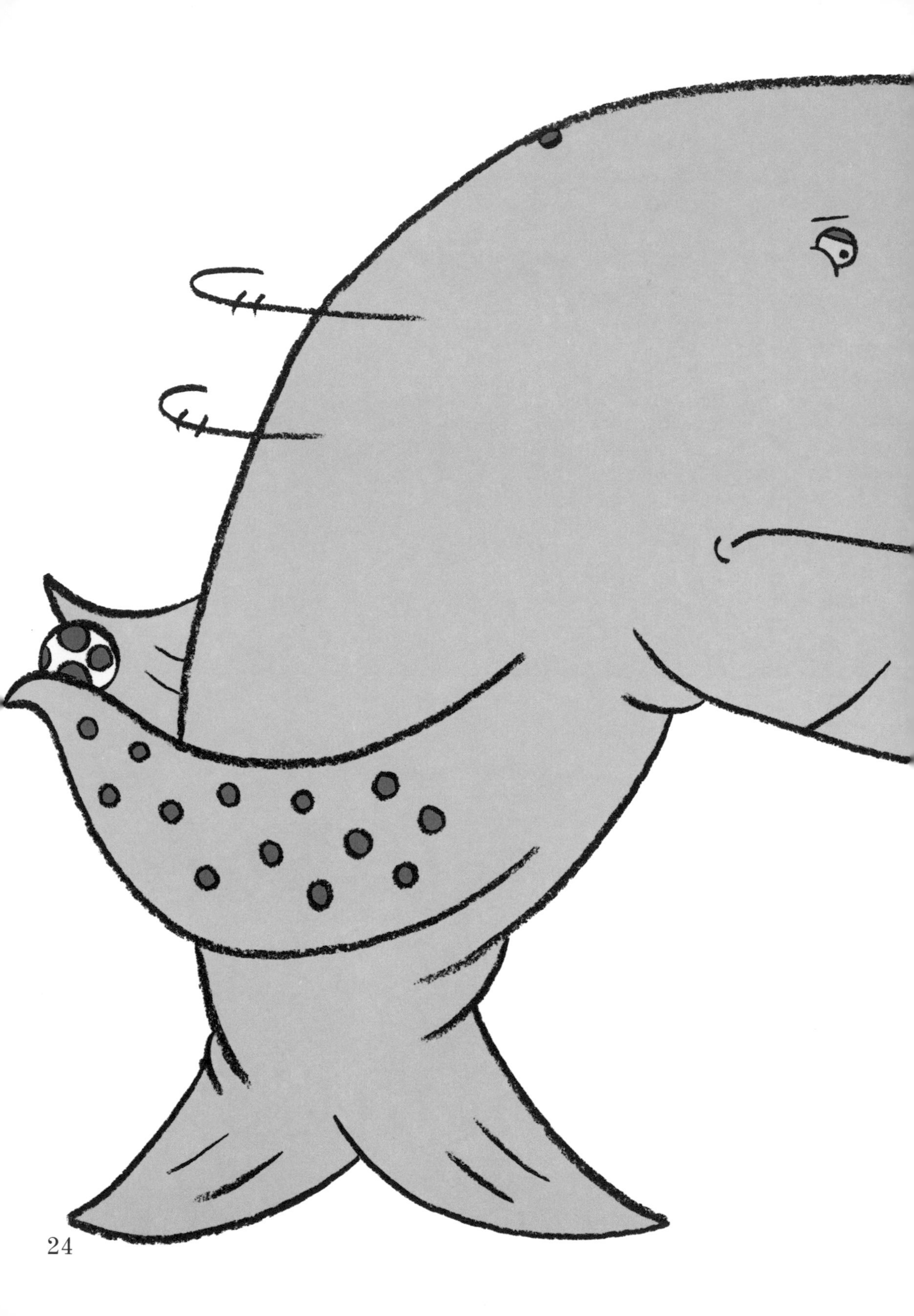

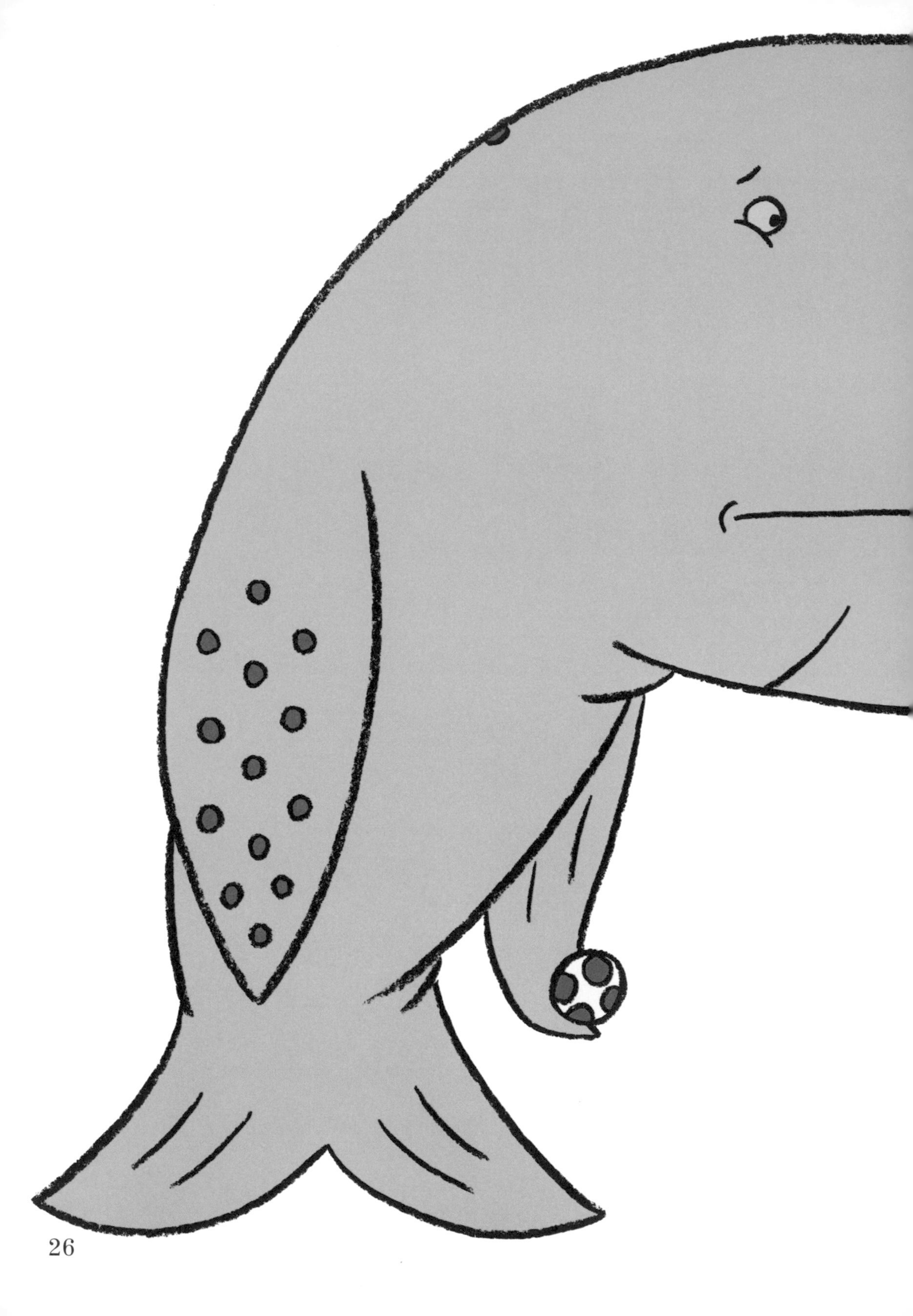

Did you get
my ball back?

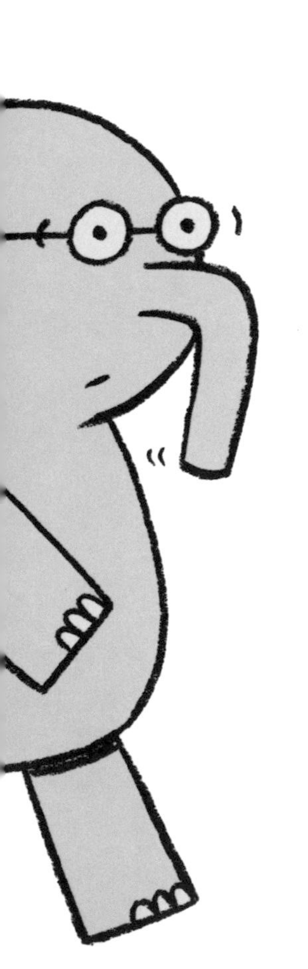

That is a
BIG guy.

You did not say *how* big he was.

He is very

BIG.

He is bigger than I am.

Much bigger!

I am smaller than he is.

Much
smaller.

He is so BIGGY-
BIG- BIG-

Gerald.

You did not
get my big ball
back, did you.

I did not.

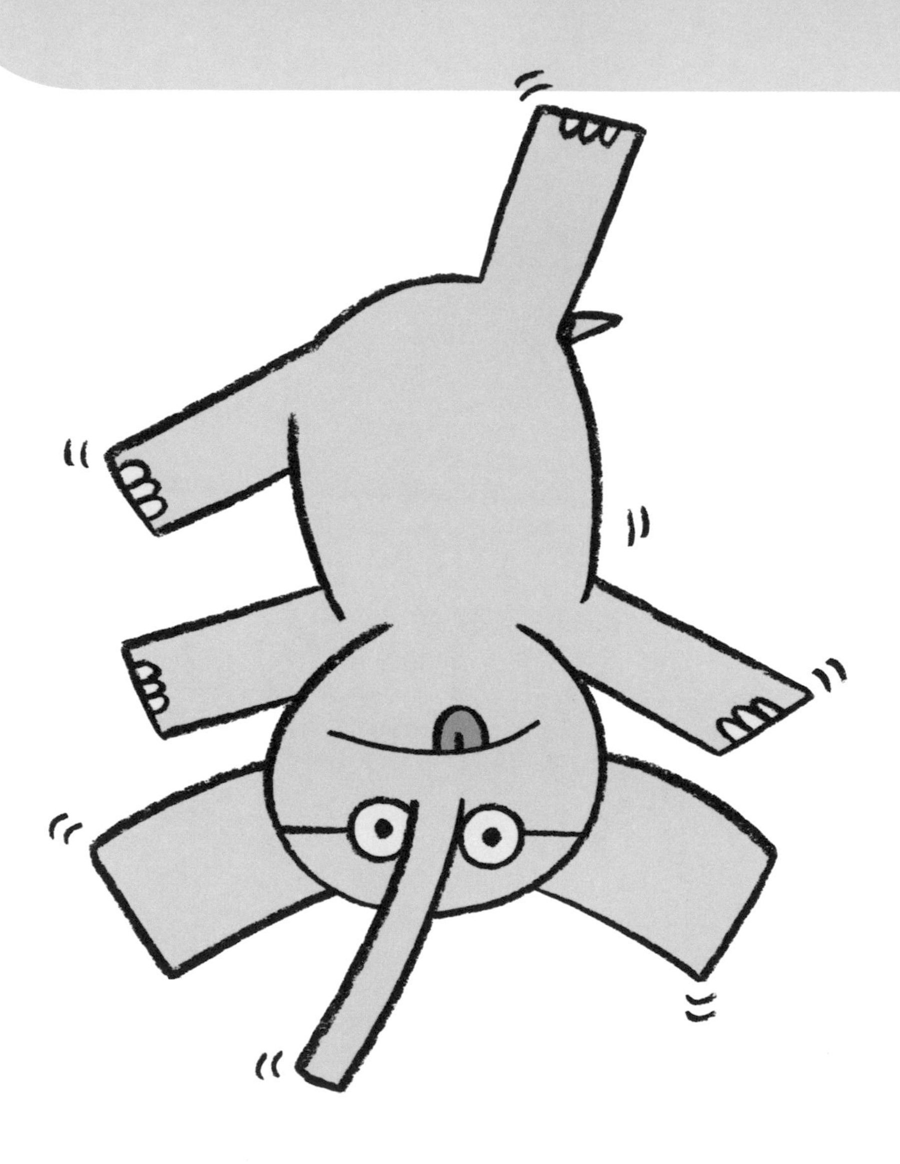
EXCUSE

ME!

THANK YOU FOR FINDING MY LITTLE BALL.

That is *your* ball?

And you think it is little?

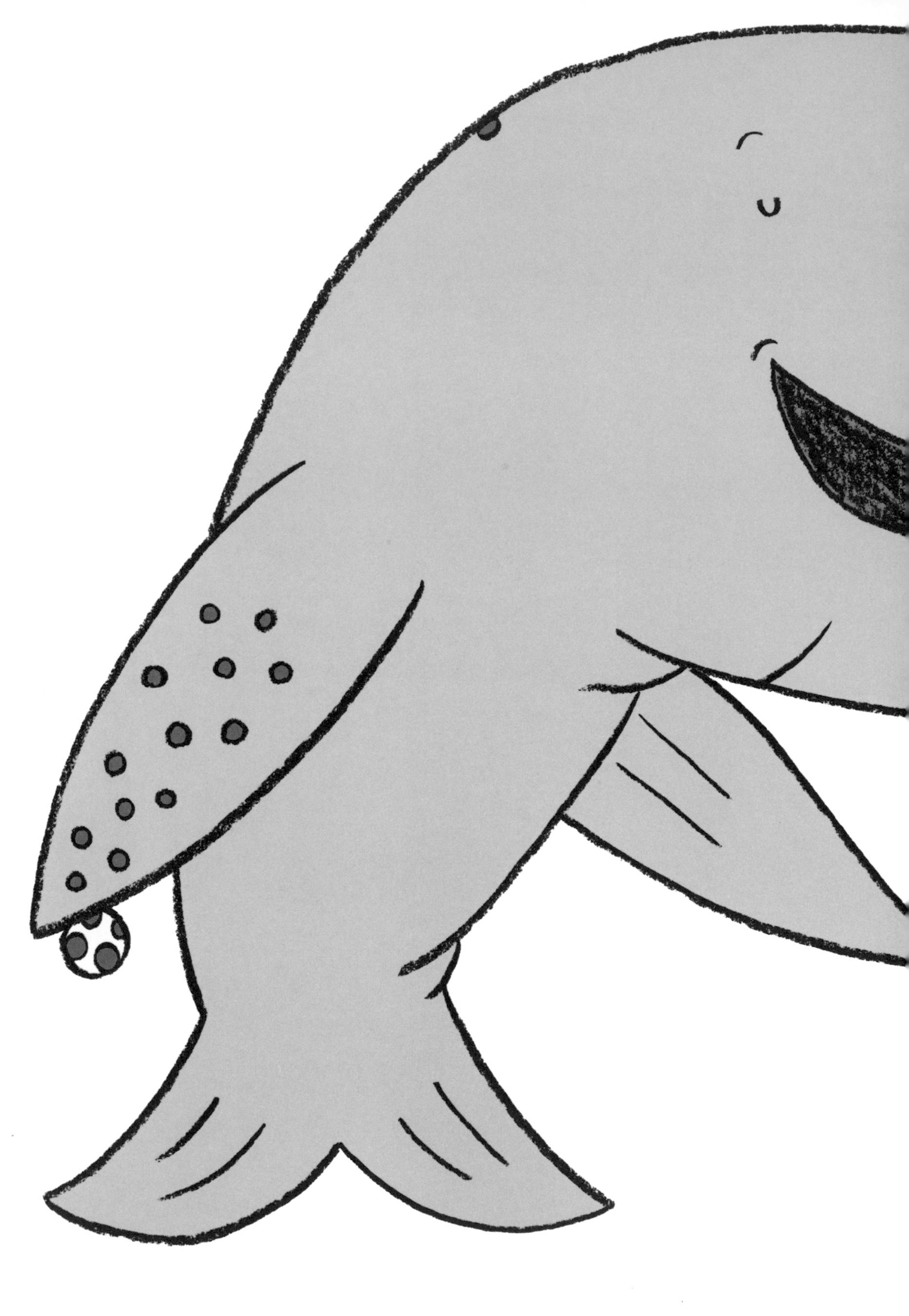

WELL,
I AM
BIG.

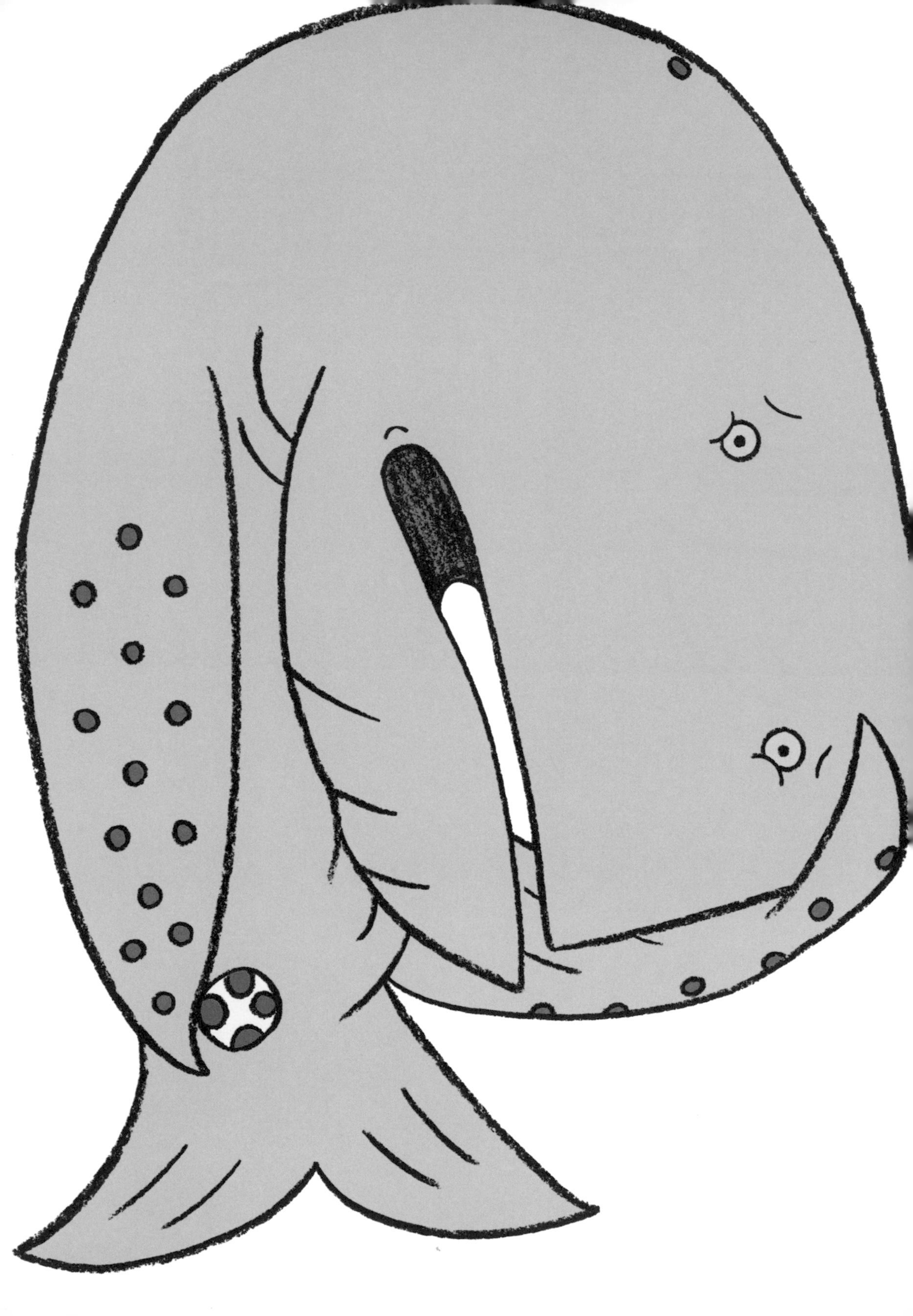

SO BIG
THAT NO
ONE WILL
PLAY
WITH ME.

LITTLE GUYS HAVE
ALL THE FUN.

Um . . .
Big Guy!
Would you
like to play
“Whale Ball”
with us?

WHAT IS "WHALE BALL"?

We do not know!

We have not made it up yet!

With a *little* help,
we can all have

BIG FUN!

Elephant and Piggie have more funny adventures in:

Today I Will Fly!

My Friend Is Sad

I Am Invited to a Party!

There Is a Bird on Your Head!
(Theodor Seuss Geisel Medal)

I Love My New Toy!

I Will Surprise My Friend!

Are You Ready to Play Outside?
(Theodor Seuss Geisel Medal)

Watch Me Throw the Ball!

Elephants Cannot Dance!

Pigs Make Me Sneeze!

I Am Going!

Can I Play Too?

We Are in a Book!
(Theodor Seuss Geisel Honor)

I Broke My Trunk!
(Theodor Seuss Geisel Honor)

Should I Share My Ice Cream?

Happy Pig Day!

Listen to My Trumpet!

Let's Go for a Drive!